The Bailey Triplets
and the Money Lesson
Bobby, Betsy, Betty, Purrypaws, and Pupdog

by Pamela Bell

Illustrated by Penny Weber

Dedication

Once again ...
With love for my cherished grandchildren ... Lloyd, Violetta, Gianna, Delila and Dylan ... who so loved Grammy's storytelling, but especially dedicated to the triplets who were the inspiration for a series of stories about identical twin girls and their triplet brother. If not for them, the stories would never have happened. Now you finally have Grammy's stories in real books, and though they have unfortunately come later than I wanted, I hope that they'll be cherished, so that one day you'll be reading them to your own children and grandchildren, and perhaps they'll read them to theirs.

To my loving daughter, Courtney, who urged me to try writing the grandchildren's favorite story of the hundreds I told them at nap time, as they sweetly snuggled in their sleeping bags. Because of you and your never ending encouragement and belief in my ability, plus our lifelong love of storybooks that rhyme, the series was born. Without your persistence, the first story would have never been written to inspire the idea of an entire series. You were always my driving force because of your constant love, support and vision throughout, so I lovingly attribute and share the accomplishment with you.

To my dearest friend, Candace, whose vivid imagination and enthusiasm led to hours upon hours of long distance brainstorming. You contributed greatly to the story ideas and the humor and moral lesson each conveys. You constantly reenforced my confidence in their potential to teach children important lessons while still captivating them with rhyme. The stories are a part of you and better because of you.

To Cora, in loving memory of our fifty-seven year friendship, for your many hours spent eagerly listening to my stories, offering valuable feedback and for your unwavering belief in their appeal and in me. I will always love and miss you, hoping and wondering if you are reading in heaven.

For my loving daughter, Ashley, who from a very young age was obsessed with all stories that rhymed, could almost flawlessly recite her favorite, "The Night Before Christmas", and never got enough of Dr Seuss. Now you can revisit and enjoy that childhood obsession, reading the stories to dear "Silly Dilly", who is the perfect age to enjoy them.

YOU ARE ALL THE MOST IMPORTANT PEOPLE IN MY LIFE
AND I LOVE YOU WITH ALL MY HEART

It was only one week before Halloween,
And the Bailey triplets could hardly wait,
As they anxiously checked their calendar,
And slid their spider toward the date.

Bobby's costume was a spiffy skeleton,
Wearing a silk vest and a tall top hat.

Betty's was a pink ballerina,

And Betsy's was a big, black, long-tailed cat.

When they put on their costumes to show their dad,
Pupdog got spooked and hid under the chair,
While Purrypaws just laid purring,
On the comfy arm without a care.

Tonight they were carving pumpkins,
And spooking up the house outside and in.
Their mom was making pumpkin treats,
And someone's pumpkin design would win.

They had each put in a dollar,
And so did their mother and dad.
Then their grammy added five,
So ten dollars could be had.

Their grammy would pick the winner,
But couldn't know who the carvers were,
And Betsy was desperate to win it,
Cause she needed ten bucks for sure!

On their birthday their parents had surprised them,
When they poured a toast and said, "It's time,
The three of you get a weekly allowance,
And learn the value of a dime.

"You'll have to learn to budget,
Deciding what's important and not,
And we'll be spending less on you,
So that managing money gets taught."

And then, they clearly warned them,
"If your loot for the week gets spent,
They'll be no money till Friday,
No matter what or where it went."

It was wonderful earning money,
And having it to spend,
But Betsy's was always gone,
Before the week came to an end.

She simply loved to buy things,
And could never tell herself no,
Like candy and gum and frivolous stuff,
And her money would quickly go.

Betty was a stasher and a thrifty spender.
She loved bargains and saving for things,
Always counting and stashing her cash,
In a hidden drawer beneath her rings.

Bobby was a practical spender.
He would save about a third.
The rest he spent quite wisely,
But Betsy's spending was absurd!

Their field trip to the amusement park,
Was right around the corner,
And if she didn't have ten dollars,
She wouldn't go, her mother warned her.

So all month long she planned her pumpkin,
Keeping it a secret all the while,
Certain that the big plump pumpkin cat,
Would make her Grammy smile.

When nighttime came, they all got to work.
Bobby and their dad spooked up the outside,
With cackling witches,
black lights and skeletons,
And some eerie music to coincide.

Their mother and the girls decorated indoors,
Posing their collection of zombie dolls,
And hung strings of skeleton lights,
That cast eerie images on the walls.

When Pup and Paws got a glimpse of the dolls,
Paws arched up her back like a Halloween cat,
Pup tucked his tail and his hackles stood up,
And they frantically fled in a lightning scat!

Then it was time for carving,
And they each took their carving seat,
In front of their perfectly chosen pumpkins,
And designing tools displayed all neat.

Bobby made a pumpkin mummy,
All wrapped up and glued in gauze,
With big black holes for eyes,
But, only the gauze, got applause

Betty made a princessy pumpkin,
Painted pink and topped with a crown,
With glued on jewels for lips and eyes,
But, the lack of carving, got a frown.

Betsy made a pumpkin cat masterpiece,
With glowing gold marbles embedded for eyes,
And an open mouth with fangs and whiskers,
That won the carving prize!

Then they all displayed their pumpkin heads,
But Betty and Bobby looked a bit forlorn,
Till they decided their sister deserved to win,
And happily ate caramel apples and candy corn.

When Halloween came, they got on their costumes,
And took their treat bags and money to the school fair,
To play all the booth games and trick-or-treat,
And see if the haunted cave would scare.

Their mother bought them rolls of tokens,
But the tokens went fast on the games and the cave,
And when they'd spent the very last one,
Betsy suggested buying more with the money they saved.

Their mother stood silently and listened,
Curious what each one would decide,
Since they were the boss of their money,
And she was no longer their guide.

Betty said, "No, I've had enough fun."
And Bobby said, "I'll only part with four."
Betsy splurged, and spent six bucks,
And the two went in the cave some more.

When the carnival was about to close,
They begged their mom for a cotton candy to go.
Their mom said, "It's not in the budget,"
But Betsy had to have one and spent her dough.

At home, when she emptied her treat bag,
All her dollars were spent, except two.
But, in bed, she thought of the fun she had,
And, dozing off, didn't even feel blue.

The next day, when Ice Cream
Chucky's truck rolled by,
Betty and Bobby bought the pops
 that were cheap,
But Betsy had to have the
Chucky's cup,
A deluxe that was three scoops deep!

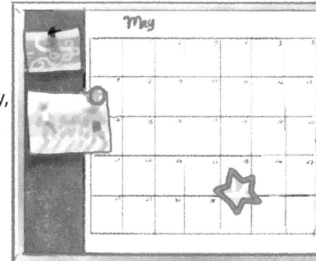

When the field trip was three days away,
They stuck their star on top of the date,
And then ran to remind their mother,
Cause the three could hardly wait!

She asked, "Do all of you have your ten dollars?"
And Betty and Bobby both said, "Yes."
Betsy hung her head down and mumbled,
"No. I'll have to pay it back, I guess."

Her mom said, "Oh no, my dear. That wasn't the deal.
To go, you had to contribute ten.
I'm sorry you spent all your money.
You'll have to stay with your father then."

Betsy stormed to her room and cried and cried,
But her mother would not give in.
Then Betty and Bobby felt so bad,
They each gave her a five dollar fin.

Excitedly, she ran to show her mother,
But her mom scolded her really bad!
"Give the money back, this instant!
Your attitude stinks and
 it makes me mad!"

"In this family if we can't afford it,
We don't buy it or we don't go!
We don't take or borrow money.
We save and just say no!"

"Now, go to your room and ponder
How you got in this predicament,
The times you couldn't deny yourself,
And how all your money was spent!"

This time, Betsy cried nonstop,
Humiliated, sad and distraught,
Till she finally realized her thinking,
Was the thing that was at fault.

She needed to change how she thought about money.
Her money had value that called for respect,
And learning to tell herself no,
Was the main thinking she had to correct.

Then, just like a light switching on,
Her brain fired up and she had a plan.
In two days she'd earn the money,
With a Bailey's lemonade stand.

She went to apologize and tell the plan to her mother,
And they tightly hugged and made lemonade,
Then set up a stand and flashy sign,
With five jugs of "ade" in every shade.

They made it in pink and purple,
Orange and blue and green,
And the different colors were such a hit,
That they had the longest line you've ever seen!

Baileys Lemonade In Rainbow Colors,
Made a grand thirty-six dollars that day,
And the triplets were the talk of the neighborhood,
Because lemonade had never been made that way!

With twelve dollars in each of their pockets,
Their mom let them go to the mall.
Bobby bought a target and darts,
And Betty bought a bargain doll.

Betsy, who would usually buy plenty,
With ease, proudly told herself no,
But gave her mother the ten trip dollars,
And her mother said, "I love you so."

And then Betsy held up her last two dollars,
Announcing, happy and proud as could be,
"These last two dollars will grow and grow,
Just you watch and see!"

And from that day on, they nicknamed her, Money Pots,
Cause she had a saving pot for a rainy day,
A second pot for special things,
And a third she could spend any way.

She had learned the money lesson.
She would always be saving some,
Deciding what was important,
And spend the rest on having fun.

THE END

ALWAYS SAVE SOME OF YOUR MONEY,
AND DON'T BORROW, CAUSE THEN YOU'LL OWE.
YOU'LL STILL HAVE PLENTY TO SPEND,
AND YOU'LL WATCH YOUR MONEY GROW.

Pamela Bell lives in Las Vegas, Nevada and is the grandmother of five. All of her life she had a passion for poetry and storytelling, so when her first grandchildren, the triplets, were born she began making up stories at nap time as a way to calm and entertain three rambunctious triplets and get them to fall asleep.

It worked so well, that once they were too old for naps, they continued begging to still climb into their cozy sleeping bags and listen to their Grammy's stories.

"The Lazy Lesson", by far, was their favorite story of the hundreds their grandmother made up, so several years later at the urging of her daughter, she wrote the story. It inspired the idea of an entire series about triplet adventures that would entertain, yet teach important lessons with sentiment, humor and rhyme, so that children and their parents would enjoy reading them and look forward to every lesson.

THE FIVE GRANDCHILDREN

Penny Weber is a full time illustrator from Long Island, New York. She works on Photoshop creating digital paintings and has illustrated many picture books for the trade and educational markets.

Penny lives with her husband, three children and their fat cat Tiger.